MORE SPECIAL OFFERS
FOR MR MEN AND LITTLE MISS READERS

In every Mr Men and Little Miss book like this one, and now in the Mr Men sticker and activity books, you will find a special token. Collect six tokens and we will send you a gift of your choice

Choose either a Mr Men or Little Miss poster, or a Mr Men or Little Miss **double sided** full colour bedroom door hanger.

Return this page **with six tokens per gift required** to:

Marketing Dept., MM / LM, World International Ltd.,
PO Box 7, Manchester, M19 2HD

Your name:_____

Address: _____

_____

_____

Parent / Guardian Name (Please Print)_____

|← 100 mm →|

RANCE FEE
SAUSAGES

250 mm

MR. GREEDY

Please tape a 20p coin to your request to cover part post and package cost

I enclose <u>six</u> tokens per gift, and 20p please send me:-

Posters:-	Mr Men Poster ☐	Little Miss Poster ☐
Door Hangers -	Mr Nosey / Muddle ☐	Mr Greedy / Lazy ☐
	Mr Tickle / Grumpy ☐	Mr Slow / Busy ☐
	Mr Messy / Quiet ☐	Mr Perfect / Forgetful ☐
	L Miss Fun / Late ☐	L Miss Helpful / Tidy ☐
	L Miss Busy / Brainy ☐	L Miss Star / Fun ☐

Please Tick Appropriate Box

20p

Stick 20p here please

We may occasionally wish to advise you of other Mr Men gifts.
If you would rather we didn't please tick this box ☐

Collect six of these tokens
You will find one inside every
Mr Men and Little Miss book
which has this special offer.

1 TOKEN

Offer open to residents of UK, Channel Isles and Ireland only

Mr Men and Little Miss Library Presentation Boxes

In response to the many thousands of requests for the above, we are delighted to advise that these are now available direct from ourselves,
for only **£4.99** (inc VAT) plus 50p p&p.
The full colour boxes accommodate each complete library. They have an integral carrying handle as well as a neat stay closed fastener.
Please do not send cash in the post. Cheques should be made payable to **World International Ltd. for the sum of £5.49** (inc p&p) per box.

Please note books are not included.

Please return this page with your cheque, stating below which presentation box you would like, to:-
**Mr Men Office, World International
PO Box 7, Manchester, M19 2HD**

Your name:_____

Address: _____

_____

_____Postcode: _____

Name of Parent/Guardian (please print):_____

Signature:_____

I enclose a cheque for £_____ made payable to World International Ltd.,

Please send me a Mr Men Presentation Box ☐

               Little Miss Presentation Box ☐   (please tick or write in quantity) and allow 28 days for delivery

Thank you

Offer applies to UK, Eire & Channel Isles only

MR. TALL

by Roger Hargreaves

WORLD INTERNATIONAL

Mr Tall was very very very tall.

Quite the tallest person you've ever met.

In fact, quite the tallest person you've never met, because you've never met anybody with legs as long as Mr Tall's legs.

Have you?

Now, the problem with being as tall as Mr Tall, meant that life was just one long problem.

As you can see!

"Oh dear," he used to sigh.

"Oh dear me! I do so wish that my legs weren't quite so very very very long."

He decided to go for a walk to think over his problem.

He was just stepping over a tree when he heard a voice.

A little voice.

"Hello!"

It was Mr Small, standing underneath a daisy.

But Mr Tall was so tall he couldn't see him.

So Mr Small shouted at the top of his voice.

"Hello!"

A Mr Small shout is about as loud as a bee's sneeze.

So, it took quite some time for Mr Tall to spot him.

"Oh," he said gloomily. "It's you."

"You don't look very happy," said Mr Small. "What's up?"

"I am," replied Mr Tall. "Because of these silly long legs of mine."

"Oh," said Mr Small.

Mr Small decided to cheer him up.

"Let's go for a walk together," he suggested.

So they did, which of course didn't work.

It was like a giraffe going for a walk with a mouse!

Then Mr Small had an idea.

Which did work!

And, because of the length of Mr Tall's legs, they very quickly walked all the way to the seaside.

"Come for a swim," cried Mr Small.

"Can't," replied Mr Tall. "By the time it gets deep enough for me to swim I'll be out the other side."

So Mr Small went for a swim, while Mr Tall sat down with a face which was nearly as long as his legs.

Mr Tickle came along.

"Hello," he said. "You look as if you need cheering up. Care for a tickle?"

"No thanks," replied Mr Tall. "What I would care for are some different legs. Mine are much too long."

"So are my arms," said Mr Tickle cheerfully. "But all the better for tickling!"

And off he went, chuckling, looking for somebody to tickle.

Looking for anybody to tickle!

Mr Nosey came along.

"Cheer up," he said. "You look very down in the mouth. What's the problem?"

"It's my legs," replied Mr Tall. "They're too long!"

"So's my nose," replied Mr Nosey, laughing. "But all the better for poking into other people's business!"

And he went off, looking for something to be nosey about.

Looking for anything to be nosey about.

Mr Greedy came along.

"Hello," he cried. "You look gloomy! What's wrong?"

"It's my legs," explained Mr Tall. "They're too big!"

"So is my tummy," replied Mr Greedy. "But all the better for filling with food!"

And off he went, licking his lips.

Mr Tall sat there and thought about Mr Tickle's arms, and Mr Nosey's nose, and Mr Greedy's tummy.

He smiled.

And then, he grinned.

And then he laughed out loud.

He looked at his legs, those very very very long legs of his.

"All the better for walking," he chuckled.

And walked home.

In four minutes.

Forty miles!

Mr Small came out of the sea after his short swim.

"And how am I going to get home?" he asked himself.

So, he set off walking.

All the way home.

Forty miles!

That was last year.

He got home yesterday!